I0648516

James Thomson

Spring

James Thomson

Spring

ISBN/EAN: 9783337374082

Printed in Europe, USA, Canada, Australia, Japan

Cover: Foto ©Andreas Hilbeck / pixelio.de

More available books at **www.hansebooks.com**

SPRING

BY

JAMES THOMSON

ILLUSTRATED

———•◆•———

𝔅𝔬𝔰𝔱𝔬𝔫

ESTES AND LAURIAT

PUBLISHERS

Typography by J S. Cushing & Co., Boston.

Presswork by Berwick & Smith, Boston.

SPRING.

COME. gentle Spring, ethereal mildness,
    come ;
And from the bosom of yon dropping cloud.
While music wakes around, veiled in a shower
Of shadowing roses, on our plains descend.
    O Hertford. fitted or to shine in courts
With unaffected grace. or walk the plain

The Seasons.

With innocence and meditation joined
In soft assemblage, listen to my song,
Which thy own season paints; when nature
    all
Is blooming and benevolent like thee.
    And see where surly Winter passes off,
Far to the north, and calls his ruffian blasts:
His blasts obey, and quit the howling hill,
The shattered forest, and the ravaged vale;
Wh"   .er gales succeed, at whose kind
    .ouch,
     olving snows in livid torrents lost, .
 he mountains lift their green heads to the
    sky.
    As yet the trembling year is unconfirmed,
And Winter oft at eve resumes the breeze,
Chills the pale morn, and bids his driving
    sleets
Deform the day delightless: so that scarce
The bittern knows his time, with bill ingulfed,
To shake the sounding marsh; or from the
    shore
The plovers when to scatter o'er the heath,
And sing their wild notes to the listening
    waste.   8

Spring.

At last from Aries rolls the bounteous sun,
And the bright bull receives him. Then no
    more
The expansive atmosphere is cramped with
    cold :
But, full of life and vivifying soul,
Lifts the light clouds sublime, and spreads
    them thin,
Fleecy, and white, o'er all-surrounding heaven·
Forth fly the tepid airs : and   ·fined,
Unbinding earth, the moving soft.   ·s.
Joyous, the impatient husbandman p.   ,
Relenting nature, and his lusty steers
Drives from their stalls, to where the well-
    used plough
Lies in the furrow, loosened from the frost.
There, unrefusing, to the harnessed yoke
They lend their shoulder, and begin their
    toil,
Cheered by the simple song and soaring lark.
Meanwhile incumbent o'er the shining share
The master leans, removes the obstructing
    clay,
Winds the whole work, and sidelong lays the
    glebe.   9

White, through the neighbouring fields the
    sower stalks,
With measured step; and, liberal, throws the
    grain
Into the faithful bosom of the ground:
The harrow follows harsh, and shuts the
    scene.
    Be gracious, Heaven! for now laborious
    man
Has done his part. Ye fostering breezes,
    blow!
Ye softening dews, ye tender showers, de-
    scend!
And temper all, thou world-reviving sun,
Into the perfect year! Nor ye who live
In luxury and ease, in pomp and pride,
Think these last themes unworthy of your
    ear:
Such themes as these the rural Maro sung
To wide-imperial Rome, in the full height
Of elegance and taste, by Greece refined.
In ancient times the sacred plough employed
The kings and awful fathers of mankind:
And some, with whom compared your insect-
    tribes   10

Spring.

Are but the beings of a summer's day,
Have held the scale of empire, ruled the storm
Of mighty war; then, with victorious hand,
Disdaining little delicacies, seized
The plough, and, greatly independent, scorned
All the vile stores corruption can bestow.
    Ye generous Britons, venerate the plough;
And o'er your hills, and long withdrawing
        vales,
Let Autumn spread his treasures to the sun,
Luxuriant and unbounded!   As the sea,
Far through his azure turbulent domain,
Your empire owns, and from a thousand shores
Wafts all the pomp of life into your ports;
So with superior boon may your rich soil,
Exuberant, Nature's better blessings pour
O'er every land, the naked nations clothe,
And be the exhaustless granary of a world!
    Nor only through the lenient air this change,
Delicious, breathes; the penetrative sun,
His force deep-darting to the dark retreat
Of vegetation, sets the steaming power
At large, to wander o'er the vernant earth,
In various hues; but chiefly thee, gay green,

The Seasons.

Thou smiling nature's universal robe !
United light and shade ! where the sight
    dwells
With growing strength and ever-new delight.
    From the moist meadow to the withered
    hill,
Led by the breeze, the vivid verdure runs,
And swells and deepens to the cherished eye.
The hawthorn whitens : and the juicy groves
Put forth their buds, unfolding by degrees,
Till the whole leafy forest stands displayed,
In full luxuriance, to the sighing gales ;
Where the deer rustle through the twining
    brake,
And the birds sing concealed. At once,
    arrayed
In all the colours of the flushing year,
By nature's swift and secret working hand,
The garden glows, and fills the liberal air
With lavish fragrance ; while the promised
    fruit
Lies yet a little embryo, unperceived,
Within its crimson folds.   Now from the town
Buried in smoke and sleep and noisome damps,

Spring.

Oft let me wander o'er the dewy fields,
Where freshness breathes,

And dash the trembling drops
From the bent bush, as through the verdant
    maze

The Seasons.

Of sweetbrier hedges I pursue my walk ;
Or taste the smell of dairy ; or ascend
Some eminence, Augusta, in thy plains,
And see the country, far diffused around,
One boundless blush, one white-empurpled
    shower
Of mingled blossoms ; where the raptured eye
Hurries from joy to joy, and, hid beneath
The fair profusion, yellow Autumn spies.
    If, brushed from Russian wilds, a cutting
        gale
Rise not, and scatter from his humid wings
The clammy mildew : or, dry-blowing, breathe
Untimely frost ; before whose baleful blast
The full-blown Spring through all her foliage
        shrinks,
Joyless and dead, a wide-dejected waste.
For oft, engendered by the hazy North,
Myriads on myriads, insect-armies waft
Keen in the poisoned breeze ; and wasteful eat,
Through buds and bark, into the blackened
        core,
Their eager way.   A feeble race, yet oft
The sacred sons of vengeance ; on whose
        course   16

Spring.

Corrosive famine waits, and kills the year.
To check this plague, the skilful farmer chaff
And blazing straw before his orchard burns ;
Till, all involved in smoke, the latent foe
From every cranny suffocated falls ;
Or scatters o'er the blooms the pungent dust
Of pepper, fatal to the frosty tribe ;
Or, when the envenomed leaf begins to curl,
With sprinkled water drowns them in their
     nest ;
Nor, while they pick them up with busy bill,
The little trooping birds unwisely scares.
   Be patient, swains ; these cruel-seeming
     winds
Blow not in vain. Far hence they keep, re-
     pressed,
Those deepening clouds on clouds, surcharged
     with rain,
That, o'er the vast Atlantic hither borne,
In endless train, would quench the summer-
     blaze,
And, cheerless, drown the crude unripened
     year.
   The Northeast spends his rage ; and now,
    shut up   17

The Seasons.

Within his iron caves, the effusive South
Warms the wide air, and o'er the void of heaven
Breathes the big clouds with vernal showers
    distent.
At first a dusky wreath they seem to rise,
Scarce staining ether; but by fast degrees,
In heaps on heaps, the doubling vapour sails
Along the loaded sky, and, mingling deep,
Sits on the horizon round a settled gloom:
Not such as wintry storms on mortals shed,
Oppressing life: but lovely, gentle, kind,
And full of every hope and every joy,
The wish of Nature.   Gradual sinks the breeze
Into a perfect calm; that not a breath
Is heard to quiver through the closing woods,
Or rustling turn the many-twinkling leaves
Of aspen tall.   The uncurling floods, diffused
In glassy breadth, seem through delusive lapse
Forgetful of their course.   'T is silence all,
And pleasing expectation.   Herds and flocks
Drop the dry sprig, and, mute-imploring, eye
The falling verdure.   Hushed in short sus-
    pense,
The plumy people streak their wings with oil.

18

Spring.

To throw the lucid moisture trickling off:
And wait the approaching sign to strike, at
    once,
Into the general choir.   Even mountains,
    vales,   19

The Seasons.

And forests seem, impatient, to demand
The promised sweetness.   Man superior walks
Amid the glad creation, musing praise,
And looking lively gratitude.   At last,
The clouds consign their treasures to the fields,
And, softly shaking on the dimpled pool
Prelusive drops, let all their moisture flow,
In large effusion, o'er the freshened world.
The stealing shower is scarce to patter heard,
By such as wander through the forest-walks,
Beneath the umbrageous multitude of leaves.
But who can hold the shade, while heaven de-
    scends
In universal bounty, shedding herbs
And fruits and flowers on Nature's ample lap?
Swift fancy fired anticipates their growth ;
And, while the milky nutriment distils,
Beholds the kindling country colour round.
    Thus all day long the full-distended clouds
Indulge their genial stores, and well-showered
    earth
Is deep enriched with vegetable life ;
Till, in the western sky, the downward sun
Looks out, effulgent, from amid the flush

Spring.

Of broken clouds, gay-shifting to his beam.
The rapid radiance instantaneous strikes
The illumined mountain, through the forest-
    streams,
Shakes on the floods, and in a yellow mist,
Far smoking o'er the interminable plain,
In twinkling myriads lights the dewy gems.
Moist, bright, and green, the landskip laughs
    around.
Full swell the woods ; their every music wakes,
Mixed in wild concert, with the warbling
    brooks
Increased, the distant bleatings of the hills,
The hollow lows responsive from the vales,
Whence, blending all, the sweetened zephyr
    springs.
Meantime, refracted from yon eastern cloud,
Bestriding earth, the grand ethereal bow
Shoots up immense ; and every hue unfolds,
In fair proportion, running from the red
To where the violet fades into the sky.
Here, awful Newton, the dissolving clouds
Form, fronting on the sun, thy showery prism ;
And to the sage-instructed eye unfold

The Seasons.

The various twine of light, by thee disclosed
From the white mingling maze. Not so the
    swain ;
He, wondering, views the bright enchantment
    bend.
Delightful, o'er the radiant fields, and runs
To catch the falling glory : but, amazed,
Beholds the amusive arch before him fly,
Then vanish quite away. Still night succeeds,
A softened shade, and saturated earth
Awaits the morning beam, to give to light,
Raised through ten thousand different plastic
    tubes,
The balmy treasures of the former day.
    Then spring the living herbs, profusely wild
O'er all the deep-green earth, beyond the
    power
Of botanist to number up their tribes :
Whether he steals along the lonely dale,
In silent search : or through the forest, rank
With what the dull incurious weeds account,
Bursts his blind way ; or climbs the mountain
    rock,
Fired by the nodding verdure of its brow.

Spring.

With such a liberal hand has Nature flung
Their seeds abroad, blown them about in
    winds,
Innumerous mixed them with the nursing
    mould,
The moistening current, and prolific rain.
  But who their virtues can declare? Who
    pierce,
With vision pure, into these secret stores

Of health, and life, and joy? the food of man,
While yet he lived in innocence, and told
A length of golden years, unfleshed in blood,
A stranger to the savage arts of life,
Death, rapine, carnage, surfeit, and disease,
The lord, and not the tyrant, of the world.
   The first fresh dawn then waked the glad-
     dened race
Of uncorrupted man, nor blushed to see
The sluggard sleep beneath its sacred beam.
For their light slumbers gently fumed away;
And up they rose as vigorous as the sun,
Or to the culture of the willing glebe,
Or to the cheerful tendance of the flock.
Meantime the song went round; and dance
     and sport,
Wisdom and friendly talk, successive stole
Their hours away. While in the rosy vale
Love breathed his infant sighs, from anguish
     free,
And full replete with bliss; save the sweet
     pain,
That, inly thrilling, but exalts it more.
Nor yet injurious act, nor surly deed,

Spring.

Was known among these happy sons of
    Heaven;
For reason and benevolence were law.
Harmonious Nature too looked smiling on.
Clear shone the skies, cooled with eternal
    gales,
And balmy spirit all. The youthful sun
Shot his best rays, and still the gracious
    clouds
Dropped fatness down; as o'er the swelling
    mead
The herds and flocks, commixing, played se-
    cure.
This when, emergent from the gloomy wood,
The glaring lion saw, his horrid heart
Was meekened, and he joined his sullen joy.
For music held the whole in perfect peace:
Soft sighed the flute; the tender voice was
    heard,
Warbling the varied heart; the woodlands
    round
Applied their choir; and winds and waters
    flowed
In consonance. Such were those prime of
    days. 27

But now those white unblemished man-
    ners, whence
The fabling poets took their golden age,
Are found no more amid these iron times, —
These dregs of life! Now the distempered
    mind
Has lost that concord of harmonious powers
Which forms the soul of happiness ; and all
Is off the poise within : the passions all
Have burst their bounds ; and reason half ex-
    tinct,
Or impotent, or else approving, sees
The foul disorder. Senseless and deformed,
Convulsive anger storms at large ; or, pale
And silent, settles into fell revenge.
Base envy withers at another's joy,
And hates that excellence it cannot reach.
Desponding fear, of feeble fancies full,
Weak and unmanly, loosens every power.
Even love itself is bitterness of soul,
A pensive anguish pining at the heart :
Or, sunk to sordid interest, feels no more
That noble wish, that never cloyed desire,
Which, selfish joy disdaining, seeks alone

Spring.

To bless the dearer object of its flame.
Hope sickens with extravagance; and grief,
Of life impatient, into madness swells;
Or in dead silence wastes the weeping hours.
These, and a thousand mixt emotions more,
From ever-changing views of good and ill,
Formed infinitely various, vex the mind
With endless storm. Whence, deeply rank-
    ling, grows
The partial thought, a listless unconcern,
Cold, and averting from our neighbour's good;
Then dark disgust and hatred, winding wiles,
Coward deceit, and ruffian violence.
At last, extinct each social feeling, fell
And joyless inhumanity pervades
And petrifies the heart. Nature disturbed
Is deemed, vindictive, to have changed her
    course.
   Hence, in old dusky time, a deluge came:
When the deep-cleft disparting orb, that
    arched
The central waters round, impetuous rushed,
With universal burst. into the gulf,

And o'er the high-piled hills of fractured
    earth
Wide dashed the waves, in undulation vast;
Till, from the centre to the streaming clouds,
A shoreless ocean tumbled round the globe.
    The seasons since have, with severer sway,
Oppressed a broken world: the Winter keen
Shook forth his waste of snows; and Summer
    shot
His pestilential heats. Great Spring, before,
Greened all the year; and fruits and blos-
    soms blushed,
In social sweetness, on the selfsame bough.
Pure was the temperate air: an even calm
Perpetual reigned, save what the zephyrs
    bland
Breathed o'er the blue expanse: for then nor
    storms
Were taught to blow, nor hurricanes to rage;
Sound slept the waters; no sulphureous
    glooms
Swelled in the sky, and sent the lightning
    forth;
While sickly damps, and cold autumnal fogs,

Spring.

Hung not, relaxing, on the springs of life.
But now, of turbid elements the sport,
From clear to cloudy tost, from hot to cold,
And dry to moist, with inward-eating change,
Our drooping days are dwindled down to
  naught,
Their period finished ere 't is well begun.
  And yet the wholesome herb neglected
  dies ;
Though with the pure exhilarating soul
Of nutriment and health, and vital powers,
Beyond the search of art, 't is copious blest.
For, with hot ravine fired, ensanguined man
Is now become the lion of the plain,
And worse. The wolf, who from the nightly
  fold
Fierce drags the bleating prey, ne'er drunk
  her milk,
Nor wore her warming fleece : nor has the
  steer,
At whose strong chest the deadly tiger hangs,
E'er ploughed for him. They too are tem-
  pered high,
With hunger stung, and wild necessity ;

—

Nor lodges pity in their shaggy breast.
But man, whom Nature formed of milder
   clay,
With every kind emotion in his heart,
And taught alone to weep — while from her
   lap
She pours ten thousand delicacies, herbs,
And fruits, as numerous as the drops of rain
Or beams that gave them birth — shall he,
   fair form,
Who wears sweet smiles, and looks erect on
   heaven,
E'er stoop to mingle with the prowling herd,
And dip his tongue in gore? The beast of
   prey,
Blood-stained, deserves to bleed: but you,
   ye flocks,
What have ye done; ye peaceful people,
   what,
To merit death? You, who have given us
   milk
In luscious streams, and lent us your own
   coat
Against the Winter's cold? And the plain ox,

Spring.

That harmless, honest, guileless animal,
In what has he offended? He, whose toil,
Patient and ever ready, clothes the land
With all the pomp of harvest, — shall he
    bleed,
And struggling groan beneath the cruel hands
Even of the clowns he feeds? And that, per-
    haps,
To swell the riot of the autumnal feast,
Won by his labour? This the feeling heart
Would tenderly suggest : but 't is enough,
In this late age, adventurous, to have touched
Light on the numbers of the Samian sage.
High Heaven forbids the bold presumptuous
    strain,
Whose wisest Will has fixed us in a state
That must not yet to pure perfection rise.
Besides, who knows, how, raised to higher
    life,
From stage to stage, the vital scale ascends?
  Now when the first foul torrent of the
    brooks,
Swelled with the vernal rains, is ebbed away ;
And, whitening, down their mossy-tinctured
    stream   37

Descends the billowy foam; now is the time,
While yet the dark-brown water aids the guile,
To tempt the trout. The well-dissembled fly,
The rod fine-tapering with elastic spring,
Snatched from the hoary steed the floating
    line,
And all thy slender watery stores, prepare.
But let not on thy hook the tortured worm,
Convulsive, twist in agonising folds :
Which, by rapacious hunger swallowed deep,
Gives as you tear it from the bleeding breast
Of the weak, helpless, uncomplaining wretch,
Harsh pain and horror to the tender hand.
    When, with his lively ray, the potent sun
Has pierced the streams, and roused the finny
    race,
Then, issuing cheerful, to thy sport repair ;
Chief should the western breezes curling play,
And light o'er ether bear the shadowy clouds.
High to their fount, this day, amid the hills,
And woodlands warbling round, trace up the
    brooks ;
The next, pursue their rocky-channelled maze,
Down to the river, in whose ample wave

Spring.

Their little Naiads love to sport at large.
Just in the dubious point, where with the pool
Is mixed the trembling stream, or where it
      boils
Around the stone, or from the hollowd bank,

Reverted plays in undulating flow,
There throw, nice-judging, the delusive fly;
And, as you lead it round in artful curve,
With eye attentive mark the springing game.
Straight as above the surface of the flood
They wanton rise, or urged by hunger leap,
Then fix, with gentle twitch, the barbéd hook:
Some lightly tossing to the grassy bank,
And to the shelving shore slow dragging some,
With various hand proportioned to their force.
If yet too young, and easily deceived,
A worthless prey scarce bends your pliant rod,
Him, piteous of his youth, and the short space
He has enjoyed the vital light of Heaven,
Soft disengage, and back into the stream
The speckled infant throw.   But should you
       lure
From his dark haunt, beneath the tangled roots
Of pendent trees, the monarch of the brook,
Behoves you then to ply your finest art.
Long time he, following cautious, scans the fly;
And oft attempts to seize it, but as oft
The dimpled water speaks his jealous fear.
At last, while haply o'er the shaded sun

Spring.

Passes a cloud, he desperate takes the death,
With sullen plunge.   At once he darts along,
Deep-struck, and runs out all the lengthened
    line ;
Then seeks the farthest ooze, the sheltering
    weed,
The caverned bank, his old secure abode ;
And flies aloft, and flounces round the pool,
Indignant of the guile.   With yielding hand,
That feels him still, yet to his furious course
Gives way, you, now retiring, following now
Across the stream, exhaust his idle rage ;
Till floating broad upon his breathless side,
And to his fate abandoned, to the shore
You gayly drag your unresisting prize.
  Thus pass the temperate hours : but when
    the sun
Shakes from his noonday throne the scatter-
    ing clouds,
Even shooting listless languor through the
    deeps,
Then seek the bank where flowering elders
    crowd,
Where scattered wild the lily of the vale

The Seasons.

Its balmy essence breathes, where cowslips
    hang
The dewy head, where purple violets lurk,
With all the lowly children of the shade :
Or lie reclined beneath yon spreading ash,
Hung o'er the steep ; whence, borne on liquid
    wing,
The sounding culver shoots ; or where the
    hawk,
High in the beetling cliff, his eyry builds.
There let the classic page thy fancy lead
Through rural scenes ; such as the Mantuan
    swain
Paints in the matchless harmony of song ;
Or catch thyself the landskip, gliding swift
Athwart imagination's vivid eye ;
Or, by the vocal woods and waters lulled,
And lost in lonely musing, in a dream,
Confused, of careless solitude, where mix
Ten thousand wandering images of things,
Soothe every gust of passion into peace —
All but the swellings of the softened heart,
That waken, not disturb, the tranquil mind.
    Behold, yon breathing prospect bids the
        Muse   42

Throw all her beauty forth. But who can
    paint
Like Nature? Can imagination boast,
Amid its gay creation, hues like hers?
Or can it mix them with that matchless skill,
And lose them in each other, as appears
In every bud that blows? If fancy then,
Unequal, fails beneath the pleasing task,
Ah, what shall language do? Ah, where find
    words
Tinged with so many colours; and whose
    power,
To life approaching, may perfume my lays
With that fine oil, those aromatic gales,
That inexhaustive flow continual round?
    Yet, though successless, will the toil delight.
Come then, ye virgins, and ye youths, whose
    hearts
Have felt the raptures of refining love;
And thou, Amanda, come, pride of my song!
Formed by the Graces, loveliness itself !
Come with those downcast eyes, sedate and
    sweet,
Those looks demure, that deeply pierce the
    soul —   45

Where, with the light of thoughtful reason
    mixed,
Shines lively fancy and the feeling heart :
O come! and while the rosy-footed May
Steals blushing on, together let us tread
The morning dews, and gather in their prime
Fresh-blooming flowers, to grace thy braided
    hair.
And thy loved bosom that improves their
    sweets.
  See where the winding vale its lavish stores,
Irriguous, spreads. See, how the lily drinks
The latent rill, scarce oozing through the
    grass,
Of growth luxuriant; or the humid bank,
In fair profusion, decks. Long let us walk,
Where the breeze blows from yon extended
    field
Of blossomed beans. Arabia cannot boast
A fuller gale of joy than, liberal, thence
Breathes through the sense, and takes the
    ravished soul.
Nor is the mead unworthy of thy foot :
Full of fresh verdure, and unnumbered flowers,

Spring.

The negligence of Nature, wide, and wild :
Where, undisguised by mimic art, she spreads
Unbounded beauty to the roving eye.
Here their delicious task the fervent bees,
In swarming millions, tend. Around, athwart,
Through the soft air, the busy nations fly,

Cling to the bud. and, with inserted tube,
Suck its pure essence, its ethereal soul.
And oft, with bolder wing, they, soaring, dare
The purple heath, or where the wild thyme
        grows,
And yellow load them with the luscious spoil.
    At length the finished garden to the view
Its vistas opens, and its alleys green.
Snatched through the verdant maze, the hur-
        ried eye
Distracted wanders; now the bowery walk
Of covert close, where scarce a speck of day
Falls on the lengthened gloom, protracted
        sweeps;
Now meets the bending sky, the river now
Dimpling along. the breezy ruffled lake.
The forest darkening round, the glittering
        spire,
The ethereal mountain. and the distant main.
But why so far excursive? when at hand,
Along these blushing borders, bright with
        dew,
And in yon mingled wilderness of flowers,
Fair-handed Spring unbosoms every grace:

Spring.

Throws out the snowdrop and the crocus first;
The daisy, primrose, violet darkly blue,
And polyanthus of unnumbered dyes;
The yellow wall-flower, stained with iron
      brown;
And lavish stock that scents the garden round.
From the soft wing of vernal breezes shed,
Anemones; auriculas, enriched
With shining meal o'er all their velvet leaves;
And full renunculas, of glowing red.
Then comes the tulip-race, where Beauty plays
Her idle freaks: from family diffused
To family, as flies the father-dust,
The varied colours run; and, while they break
On the charmed eye, the exulting florist marks,
With secret pride, the wonders of his hand.
No gradual bloom is wanting; from the bud,
First-born of Spring, to Summer's musky
      tribes:
Nor hyacinths, of purest virgin white,
Low-bent, and blushing inward; nor jonquils,
Of potent fragrance; nor narcissus fair,
As o'er the fabled fountain hanging still;
Nor broad carnations; nor gay-spotted pinks;

Nor, showered from every bush, the damask-
    rose.
Infinite numbers, delicacies, smells,
With hues on hues expression cannot paint,
The breath of Nature, and her endless bloom.
   Hail, Source of Beings! Universal Soul
Of heaven and earth! Essential Presence,
    hail!
To Thee I bend the knee; to Thee my
    thoughts,
Continual, climb; who, with a master-hand,
Hast the great whole into perfection touched.
By Thee the various vegetative tribes,
Wrapt in a filmy net, and clad with leaves,
Draw the live ether, and imbibe the dew.
By Thee disposed into congenial soils,
Stands each attractive plant, and sucks, and
    swells
The juicy tide. — a twining mass of tubes.
At Thy command the vernal sun awakes
The torpid sap, detruded to the root
By wintry winds, that now in fluent dance,
And lively fermentation, mounting, spreads
All this innumerous-coloured scene of things.

Spring.

As rising from the vegetable world
My theme ascends, with equal wing ascend,
My panting Muse; and hark, how loud the woods
Invite you forth in all your gayest trim.
Lend me your song, ye nightingales! O, pour
The mazy-running soul of melody
Into my varied verse! while I deduce,
From the first note the hollow cuckoo sings,
The symphony of Spring, and touch a theme
Unknown to fame. — the passion of the groves.
  When first the soul of love is sent abroad,
Warm through the vital air, and on the heart
Harmonious seizes, the gay troops begin,
In gallant thought, to plume the painted wing;
And try again the long-forgotten strain,
At first faint-warbled.   But no sooner grows
The soft infusion prevalent and wide,
Than, all alive, at once their joy o'erflows
In music unconfined.   Upsprings the lark,
Shrill-voiced and loud, the messenger of morn :
Ere yet the shadows fly, he mounted sings
Amid the dawning clouds, and from their haunts

53

Calls up the tuneful nations.   Every copse
Deep-tangled, tree irregular, and bush
Bending with dewy moisture, o'er the heads
Of the coy choristers that lodge within,
Are prodigal of harmony.   The thrush
And wood-lark, o'er the kind-contending
    throng
Superior heard, run through the sweetest
    length
Of notes ; when listening Philomena deigns
To let them joy, and purposes, in thought
Elate, to make her night excel their day.
The blackbird whistles from the thorny
    brake ;
The mellow bulfinch answers from the grove :
Nor are the linnets, o'er the flowering furze
Poured out profusely, silent.   Joined to these,
Innumerous songsters, in the freshening shade
Of new-sprung leaves, their modulations mix
Mellifluous.   The jay, the rook, the daw,
And each harsh pipe, discordant heard alone,
Aid the full concert : while the stock-dove
    breathes
A melancholy murmur through the whole.

Spring.

'T is love creates their melody. and all
This waste of music is the voice of love ;
That even to birds. and beasts, the tender
    arts
Of pleasing teaches. Hence the glossy kind
Try every winning way inventive love
Can dictate, and in courtship to their mates
Pour forth their little souls. First, wide
    around.
With distant awe. in airy rings they rove.
Endeavouring by a thousand tricks to catch
The cunning, conscious. half-averted glance
Of their regardless charmer. Should she
    seem.
Softening. the least approvance to bestow.
Their colours burnish, and. by hope inspired.
They brisk advance : then, on a sudden
    struck,
Retire disordered ; then again approach :
In fond rotation spread the spotted wing.
And shiver every feather with desire.
    Connubial leagues agreed, to the deep
    woods
They haste away. all as their fancy leads.

Pleasure, or food, or secret safety prompts,
That Nature's great command may be obeyed,
For all the sweet sensations they perceive
Indulged in vain. Some to the holly-hedge
Nestling repair, and to the thicket some ;
Some to the rude protection of the thorn
Commit their feeble offspring. The cleft
    tree
Offers its kind concealment to a few,
Their food its insects, and its moss their
    nests.
Others, apart, far in the grassy dale,
Or roughening waste, their humble texture
    weave.
But most in woodland solitudes delight,
In unfrequented glooms, or shaggy banks,
Steep, and divided by a babbling brook,
Whose murmurs soothe them all the livelong
    day,
When by kind duty fixed. Among the roots
Of hazel, pendant o'er the plaintive stream,
They frame the first foundation of their
    domes ;
Dry sprigs of trees, in artful fabric laid,

And bound with clay together. Now 't is
    naught
But restless hurry through the busy air,
Beat by unnumbered wings. The swallow
    sweeps

The slimy pool, to build his hanging house
Intent. And often, from the careless back
Of herds and flocks, a thousand tugging bills
Pluck hair and wool; and oft, when unob-
    served,
Steal from the barn a straw; till soft and
    warm,
Clean and complete, their habitation grows.
    As thus the patient dam assiduous sits,
Not to be tempted from her tender task
Or by sharp hunger, or by smooth delight,
Though the whole loosened Spring around
    her blows,
Her sympathising lover takes his stand
High on the opponent bank, and ceaseless
    sings
The tedious time away; or else supplies
Her place a moment, while she sudden flits
To pick the scanty meal. The appointed
    time
With pious toil fulfilled, the callow young,
Warmed and expanded into perfect life,
Their brittle bondage break, and come to
    light;

A helpless family, demanding food
With constant clamour. O, what passions
  then,
What melting sentiments of kindly care,
On the new parents seize! Away they fly,
Affectionate, and, undesiring, bear
The most delicious morsel to their young,
Which equally distributed, again
The search begins. Even so a gentle pair,
By fortune sunk, but formed of generous
  mould,
And charmed with cares beyond the vulgar
  breast,
In some lone cot amid the distant woods,
Sustained alone by providential Heaven,
Oft, as they, weeping, eye their infant train,
Check their own appetites, and give them all.
  Nor toil alone they scorn : exalting love,
By the great Father of the Spring inspired,
Gives instant courage to the fearful race,
And to the simple, art. With stealthy wing,
Should some rude foot their woody haunts
  molest,
Amid a neighbouring bush they silent drop,

And whirring thence, as if alarmed, deceive
The unfeeling school-boy. Hence, around the
　　head
Of wandering swain, the white-winged plover
　　wheels
Her sounding flight, and then directly on
In long excursion skims the level lawn,
To tempt him from her nest. The wild-duck,
　　hence,
O'er the rough moss, and o'er the trackless
　　waste
The heath-hen flutters (pious fraud!) to lead
The hot pursuing spaniel far astray.
　　Be not the Muse ashamed, here to bemoan
Her brothers of the grove, by tyrant man
Inhuman caught, and in the narrow cage
From liberty confined, and boundless air.
Dull are the pretty slaves, their plumage dull,
Ragged, and all its brightening lustre lost ;
Nor is that sprightly wildness in their notes,
Which, clear and vigorous, warbles from the
　　beech.
O then, ye friends of love and love-taught
　　song,

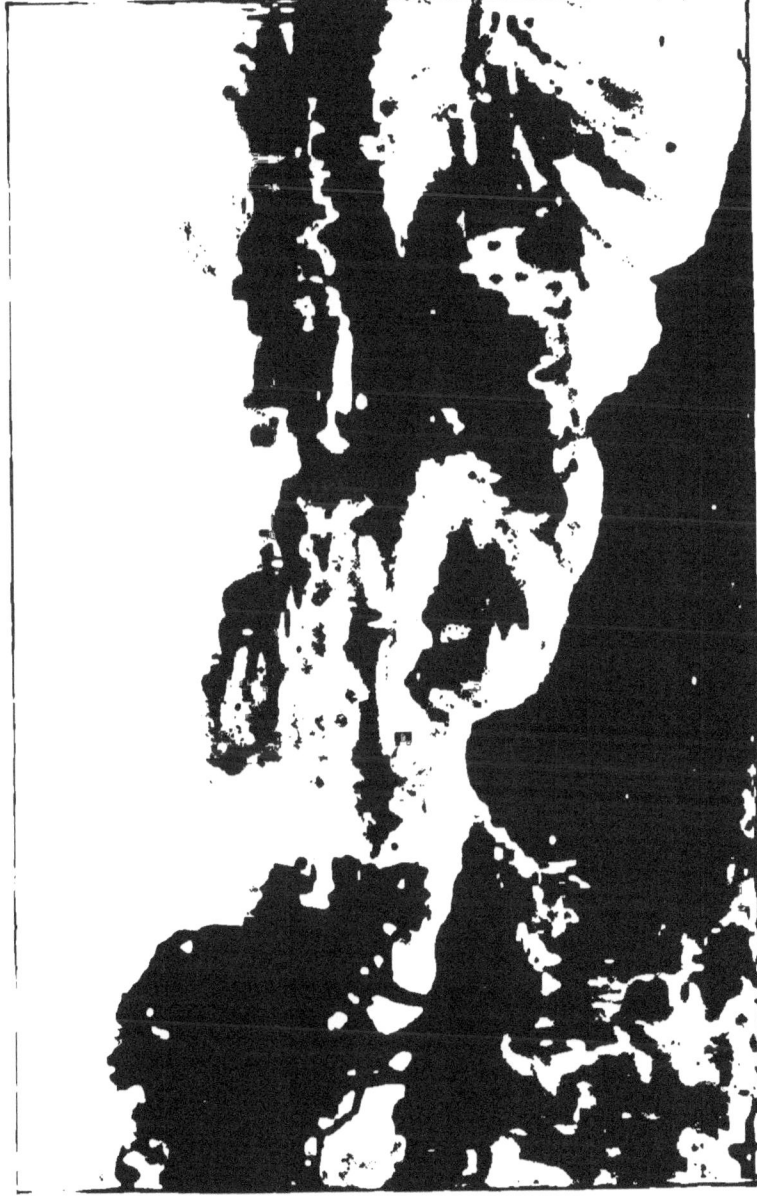

Spare the soft tribes, this barbarous art for-
     bear,
If on your bosom innocence can win,
Music engage, or piety persuade.
  But let not chief the nightingale lament
Her ruined care, too delicately framed
To brook the harsh confinement of the cage.
Oft when, returning with her loaded bill,
The astonished mother finds a vacant nest,
By the hard hand of unrelenting clowns
Robbed, to the ground the vain provision
     falls ;
Her pinions ruffle, and. low-drooping. scarce
Can bear the mourner to the poplar shade ;
Where, all abandoned to despair, she sings
Her sorrows through the night ; and, on the
     bough
Sole-sitting, still at every dying fall
Takes up again her lamentable strain
Of winding woe ; till, wide around, the woods
Sigh to her song, and with her wail resound.
  But now the feathered youth their former
     bounds.
Ardent. disdain ; and. weighing oft their
     wings,   65

Demand the free possession of the sky.
This one glad office more, and then dissolves
Parental love at once, now needless grown:
Unlavish wisdom never works in vain.
'T is on some evening, sunny, grateful, mild,
When naught but balm is breathing through
    the woods,
With yellow lustre bright, that the new tribes
Visit the spacious heavens, and look abroad
On Nature's common, far as they can see,
Or wing, their range and pasture. O'er the
    boughs
Dancing about, still at the giddy verge
Their resolution fails: their pinions still,
In loose libration stretched, to trust the void
Trembling refuse: till down before them fly
The parent guides, and chide, exhort, com-
    mand,
Or push them off. The surging air receives
The plumy burden; and their self-taught
    wings
Winnow the waving element. On ground
Alighted, bolder up again they lead,
Farther and farther on, the lengthening flight;

Till, vanished every fear, and every power
Roused into life and action, light in air
The acquitted parents see their soaring race,
And, once rejoicing, never know them more.
   High from the summit of a craggy cliff,
Hung o'er the deep, such as amazing frowns
On utmost Kilda's shore, whose lonely race
Resign the setting sun to Indian worlds,
The royal eagle draws his vigorous young,
Strong-pounced, and ardent with paternal fire.
Now fit to raise a kingdom of their own,
He drives them from his fort, the towering
      seat,
For ages, of his empire ; which, in peace,
Unstained he holds, while many a league to sea
He wings his course, and preys in distant
      isles.
   Should I my steps turn to the rural seat,
Whose lofty elms and venerable oaks
Invite the rook, who, high amid the boughs,
In early Spring, his airy city builds,
And ceaseless caws amusive ; there, well-
      pleased,
I might the various polity survey

Of the mixed household kind. The careful
    hen
Calls all her chirping family around,
Fed and defended by the fearless cock,
Whose breast with ardour flames as on he
    walks,
Graceful, and crows defiance. In the pond,
The finely checkered duck, before her train,
Rows garrulous. The stately-sailing swan
Gives out his snowy plumage to the gale;
And, arching proud his neck, with oary feet
Bears forward fierce, and guards his osier-isle,
Protective of his young. The turkey nigh,
Loud-threatening, reddens; while the peacock
    spreads
His every-coloured glory to the sun,
And swims in radiant majesty along.
O'er the whole homely scene, the cooing dove
Flies thick in amourous chase, and wanton
    rolls
The glancing eye, and turns the changeful
    neck.
    While thus the gentle tenants of the shade
Indulge their purer loves, the rougher world

Spring.

Of brutes, below, rush furious into flame
And fierce desire.   Through all his lusty veins
The bull, deep-scorched, the raging passion
    feels.
Of pasture sick, and negligent of food,
Scarce seen, he wades among the yellow
    broom,
While o'er his ample sides the rambling sprays
Luxuriant shoot; or through the mazy wood
Dejected wanders, nor the inticing bud
Crops, though it presses on his careless sense.
And oft, in jealous maddening fancy wrapt,
He seeks the fight, and, idly-butting, feigns
His rival gored in every knotty trunk.
Him should he meet, the bellowing war
    begins:
Their eyes flash fury; to the hollowed earth,
Whence the sand flies, they mutter bloody
    deeds,
And groaning deep the impetuous battle mix;
While the fair heifer, balmy-breathing, near,
Stands kindling up their rage.   The trembling
    steed,
With this hot impulse seized in every nerve,

Nor heeds the rein, nor hears the sounding
thong;
Blows are not felt; but, tossing high his head,
And by the well-known joy to distant plains
Attracted strong, all wild he bursts away;
O'er rocks and woods and craggy mountains
flies;
And, neighing, on the aerial summit takes
The exciting gale; then, steep-descending,
cleaves
The headlong torrents foaming down the hills.
Even where the madness of the straitened
stream
Turns in black eddies round: such is the
force
With which his frantic heart and sinews swell.
    Nor undelighted by the boundless Spring
Are the broad monsters of the foaming deep:
From the deep ooze and gelid cavern roused,
They flounce and tumble in unwieldy joy.
Dire were the strain, and dissonant, to sing
The cruel raptures of the savage kind:
How by this flame their native wrath sublimed,
They roam, amid the fury of their heart,

Spring.

The far-resounding waste, in fiercer bands,
And growl their horrid loves. But this the
    theme
I sing, enraptured, to the British fair,

Forbids, and leads me to the mountain-brow,
Where sits the shepherd on the grassy turf,

Inhaling, healthful, the descending sun.
Around him feeds his many-bleating flock,
Of various cadence ; and his sportive lambs,
This way and that, convolved in friskful glee,
Their frolics play.   And now the sprightly
    race
Invites them forth ; when swift, the signal
    given,
They start away, and sweep the massy mound
That runs around the hill ; the rampart once
Of iron war, in ancient barbarous times,
When disunited Britain ever bled,
Lost in eternal broil : ere yet she grew
To this deep-laid indissoluble state,
Where wealth and commerce lift the golden
    head,
And, o'er our labours, liberty and law,
Impartial, watch, — the wonder of a world !
  What is this mighty breath, ye curious, say,
That, in a powerful language, felt not heard,
Instructs the fowls of heaven ; and through
    their breast
These arts of love diffuses ?   What, but God ?
Inspiring God ! who, boundless spirit all,

Spring.

And unremitting energy, pervades,
Adjusts, sustains, and agitates the whole.
He, ceaseless, works alone; and yet alone
Seems not to work, with such perfection
    framed
Is this complex, stupendous scheme of things,
But, though concealed, to every purer eye
The informing Author in his works appears:
Chief, lovely Spring, in thee, and thy soft
    scenes,
The smiling God is seen: while water, earth,
And air attest his bounty; which exalts
The brute-creation to this finer thought,
And annual melts their undesigning hearts
Profusely thus in tenderness and joy.
   Still let my song a nobler note assume,
And sing the infusive force of Spring on man;
When heaven and earth, as if contending, vie
To raise his being, and serene his soul.
Can he forbear to join the general smile
Of Nature? Can fierce passions vex his breast,
While every gale is peace, and every grove
Is melody? Hence from the bounteous walks
Of flowing Spring, ye sordid sons of earth,

Hard, and unfeeling of another's woe,
Or only lavish to yourselves, — away !
But come, ye generous minds, in whose wide
  thought,
Of all his works, creative bounty burns,
With warmest beam ; and on your open front,
And liberal eye, sits, from his dark retreat
Inviting modest want.   Nor, till invoked,
Can restless goodness wait ; your active search
Leaves no cold wintry corner unexplored ;
Like silent-working Heaven, surprising oft
The lonely heart with unexpected good.
For you the roving spirit of the wind
Blows Spring abroad ; for you the teeming
  clouds
Descend in gladsome plenty o'er the world ;
And the sun sheds his kindest rays for you,
Ye flower of human race !   In these green
  days,
Reviving Sickness lifts her languid head ;
Life flows afresh ; and young-eyed Health
  exalts
The whole creation round.   Contentment
  walks

Spring.

The sunny glade. and feels an inward bliss
Spring o'er his mind, beyond the power of
  kings
To purchase. Pure Serenity apace
Induces thought. and contemplation still.
By swift degrees the love of Nature works,
And warms the bosom ; till at last sublimed
To rapture, and enthusiastic heat,
We feel the present Deity, and taste
The joy of God to see a happy world !
 These are the sacred feelings of thy heart,
Thy heart informed by reason's purer ray,
O Lyttelton, the friend ! thy passions thus
And meditations vary, as at large,
Courting the Muse, through Hagley Park you
  stray ;
Thy British Tempé ! there along the dale.
With woods o'erhung. and shagged with
  mossy rocks,
Whence on each hand the gushing waters
  play,
And down the rough cascade white-dashing
  fall.
Or gleam in lengthened vista through the
  trees, 77

You silent steal; or sit beneath the shade
Of solemn oaks, that tuft the swelling mounts
Thrown graceful round by Nature's careless
    hand,
And pensive listen to the various voice
Of rural peace: the herds, the flocks, the
    birds,
The hollow-whispering breeze, the plaint of
    rills,
That, purling down amid the twisted roots
Which creep around, their dewy murmurs
    shake
On the soothed ear. From these abstracted
    oft,
You wander through the philosophic world;
Where in bright train continual wonders rise,
Or to the curious or the pious eye.
And oft, conducted by historic truth,
You tread the long extent of backward time.
Planning, with warm benevolence of mind,
And honest zeal unwarped by party rage,
Britannia's weal; how from the venal gulf
To raise her virtue, and her arts revive.
Or, turning thence thy view, these graver
    thoughts   78

Spring.

The Muses charm: while, with sure taste re-
    fined,
You draw the inspiring breath of ancient song,
Till nobly rises, emulous, thy own.
Perhaps thy loved Lucinda shares thy walk,
With soul to thine attuned. Then Nature
    all
Wears to the lover's eye a look of love;
And all the tumult of a guilty world,
Tost by ungenerous passions, sinks away.
The tender heart is animated peace;
And as it pours its copious treasures forth,
In varied converse, softening every theme,
You, frequent-pausing, turn, and from her
    eyes,
Where meekened sense, and amiable grace,
And lively sweetness dwell, enraptured drink
That nameless spirit of ethereal joy,
Inimitable happiness! which love
Alone bestows, and on a favoured few.
Meantime you gain the height, from whose
    fair brow
The bursting prospect spreads immense
    around;

And snatched o'er hill and dale, and wood
    and lawn,
And verdant field, and darkening heath be-
    tween,
And villages embosomed soft in trees,
And spiry towns by surging columns marked
Of household smoke, your eye excursive
    roams ;
Wide-stretching from the hall in whose kind
    haunt
The hospitable genius lingers still,
To where the broken landscape, by degrees
Ascending, roughens into rigid hills ;
O'er which the Cambrian mountains, like far
    clouds
That skirt the blue horizon, dusky, rise.
  Flushed by the spirit of the genial year,
Now from the virgin's cheek a fresher bloom
Shoots, less and less, the live carnation round ;
Her lips blush deeper sweets ; she breathes of
    youth ;
The shining moisture swells into her eyes
In brighter flow : her wishing bosom heaves,
With palpitations wild ; kind tumults seize

Her veins, and all her yielding soul is love.
From the keen gaze her lover turns away,
Full of the dear ecstatic power, and sick
With sighing languishment. Ah then, ye
    fair !
Be greatly cautious of your sliding hearts;
Dare not the infectious sigh; the pleading
    look,

Downcast and low, in meek submission
    dressed,
But full of guile. Let not the fervent tongue
Prompt to deceive, with adulation smooth,
Gain on your purposed will. Nor in the
    bower,

Where woodbines flaunt, and roses shed a
    couch,
While Evening draws her crimson curtains
    round,
Trust your soft minutes with betraying man.
  And let the aspiring youth beware of love.
Of the smooth glance beware; for 't is too
    late,
When on his heart the torrent-softness pours.
Then wisdom prostrate lies, and fading fame
Dissolves in air away : while the fond soul,
Wrapped in gay visions of unreal bliss,
Still paints the illusive form, the kindling
    grace,
The inticing smile, the modest-seeming eye,
Beneath whose beauteous beams, belying
    Heaven,
Lurk searchless cunning, cruelty, and death :
And still, false-warbling in his cheated ear,
Her siren voice, enchanting, draws him on,
To guileful shores, and meads of fatal joy.
  Even present, in the very lap of Love
Inglorious laid, — while music flows around,
Perfumes, and oils, and wine, and wanton
    hours, —   **82**

Spring.

Amid the roses, fierce Repentance rears
Her snaky crest: a quick-returning pang
Shoots through the conscious heart; where
    honour still,
And great design, against the oppressive load
Of luxury, by fits, impatient heave.
  But absent, what fantastic woes, aroused,
Rage in each thought, by restless musing fed,
Chill the warm cheek, and blast the bloom of
    life !
Neglected fortune flies ; and, sliding swift,
Prone into ruin fall his scorned affairs.
'T is naught but gloom around. The dark-
    ened sun
Loses his light. The rosy-bosomed Spring
To weeping fancy pines; and yon bright
    arch,
Contracted, bends into a dusky vault.
All Nature fades extinct ; and she alone,
Heard, felt, and seen, possesses every thought,
Fills every sense, and pants in every vein.
Books are but formal dulness, tedious friends ;
And sad amid the social band he sits,
Lonely and unattentive. From the tongue

The Seasons.

The unfinished period falls : while borne
    away,
On swelling thought, his wafted spirit flies
To the vain bosom of his distant fair ;
And leaves the semblance of a lover, fixed
In melancholy site, with head declined,
And love-dejected eyes. Sudden he starts,
Shook from his tender trance, and, restless,
    runs
To glimmering shades and sympathetic
    glooms,
Where the dun umbrage o'er the falling
    stream,
Romantic, hangs ; there through the pensive
    dusk
Strays, in heart-thrilling meditation lost,
Indulging all to love : or on the bank
Thrown, amid drooping lilies, swells the
    breeze
With sighs unceasing, and the brook with
    tears.
Thus in soft anguish he consumes the day,
Nor quits his deep retirement, till the moon
Peeps through the chambers of the fleecy
    east,   84

Spring.

Enlightened by degrees, and in her train
Leads on the gentle hours; then forth he
 walks,
Beneath the trembling languish of her beam,
With softened soul, and wooes the bird of
 eve
To mingle woes with his; or, while the world
And all the sons of care lie hushed in sleep,
Associates with the midnight shadows drear;
And, sighing to the lonely taper, pours
His idly-tortured heart into the page
Meant for the moving messenger of love;
Where rapture burns on rapture, every line
With rising frenzy fired.   But if on bed
Delirious flung, sleep from his pillow flies.
All night he tosses, nor the balmy power
In any posture finds; till the gray morn
Lifts her pale lustre on the paler wretch,
Examinate by love: and then perhaps
Exhausted nature sinks awhile to rest,
Still interrupted by distracted dreams,
That o'er the sick imagination rise,
And in black colours paint the mimic scene.
Oft with the enchantress of his soul he talks;

Sometimes in crowds distressed ; or, if retired
To secret-winding flower-enwoven bowers
Far from the dull impertinence of man,
Just as he, credulous, his endless cares
Begins to lose in blind oblivious love,
Snatched from her yielded hand, he knows
    not how,
Through forests huge, and long untravelled
    heaths
With desolation brown, he wanders waste,
In night and tempest wrapt; or shrinks
    aghast,
Back from the bending precipice ; or wades
The turbid stream below, and strives to reach
The farther shore, where, succourless and sad,
She with extended arms his aid implores ;
But strives in vain ; borne by the outrageous
    flood
To distance down, he rides the ridgy wave,
Or, whelmed beneath the boiling eddy, sinks.
These are the charming agonies of love,
Whose misery delights. But through the
    heart
Should jealousy its venom once diffuse,

Spring.

'T is then delightful misery no more,
But agony unmixed, incessant gall,
Corroding every thought, and blasting all
Love's Paradise.   Ye fairy prospects, then,
Ye beds of roses, and ye bowers of joy,
Farewell ! ye gleamings of departed peace,
Shine   out   your   last !   the   yellow-tingeing
        plague
Internal vision taints, and in a night
Of livid gloom imagination wraps.
Ah then, instead of love-enlivened cheeks,
Of sunny features, and of ardent eyes
With flowing rapture bright, dark looks suc-
        ceed,
Suffused, and glaring with untender fire, —
A clouded aspect, and a burning cheek,
Where the whole poisoned soul, malignant,
        sits,
And frightens love away.   Ten thousand
        fears
Invented wild, ten thousand frantic views
Of horrid rivals, hanging on the charms
For which he melts in fondness, eat him up
With fervent anguish and consuming rage.

In vain reproaches lend their idle aid,
Deceitful pride, and resolution frail,
Giving false peace a moment. Fancy pours,
Afresh, her beauties on his busy thought,
Her first endearments twining round the soul
With all the witchcraft of ensnaring love.
Straight the fierce storm involves his mind
     anew,
Flames through the nerves, and boils along
     the veins ;
While anxious doubt distracts the tortured
     heart :
For even the sad assurance of his fears
Were peace to what he feels. Thus the warm
     youth,
Whom love deludes into his thorny wilds,
Through flowery-tempting paths, or leads a
     life
Of fevered rapture, or of cruel care ;
His brightest aims extinguished all, and all
His lively moments running down to waste.
  But happy they, the happiest of their kind !
Whom gentler stars unite, and in one fate
Their hearts, their fortunes, and their beings
     blend.   92

Spring.

'T is not the coarser tie of human laws,
Unnatural oft, and foreign to the mind,
That binds their peace. but harmony itself,
Attuning all their passions into love ;
Where friendship full-exerts her softest power,
Perfect esteem enlivened by desire
Ineffable. and sympathy of soul ;
Thought meeting thought, and will prevent-
    ing will,
With boundless confidence : for naught but
    love
Can answer love. and render bliss secure.
Let him. ungenerous, who, alone intent
To bless himself. from sordid parents buys
The loathing virgin, in eternal care,
Well-merited, consume his nights and days ;
Let barbarous nations, whose inhuman love
Is wild desire, fierce as the suns they feel ;
Let Eastern tyrants from the light of heaven
Seclude their bosom-slaves, meanly possessed
Of a mere lifeless. violated form :
While those whom love cements in holy faith,
And equal transport. free as Nature live,
Disdaining fear. What is the world to them,

Its pomp. its pleasure, and its nonsense all !
Who in each other clasp whatever fair
High fancy forms. and lavish hearts can wish ;
Something than beauty dearer. should they
    look
Or on the mind, or mind-illumined face, —
Truth. goodness. honour. harmony, and love.
The richest bounty of indulgent Heaven.
Meantime a smiling offspring rises round.
And mingles both their graces. By degrees,
The human blossom blows ; and every day,
Soft as it rolls along. shows some new
    charm. —
The father's lustre and the mother's bloom.
Then infant reason grows apace, and calls
For the kind hand of an assiduous care.
Delightful task ! to rear the tender thought.
To teach the young idea how to shoot,
To pour the fresh instruction o'er the mind.
To breathe the enlivening spirit, and to fix
The generous purpose in the glowing breast.
O. speak the joy. ye. whom the sudden tear
Surprises often. while you look around,
And nothing strikes your eye but sights of
    bliss ;   94

Spring.

All various Nature pressing on the heart, —
An elegant sufficiency, content,
Retirement, rural quiet, friendship, books,
Ease and alternate labour, useful life,
Progressive virtue, and approving Heaven !
These are the matchless joys of virtuous love ;
And thus their moments fly.   The seasons
    thus,
As ceaseless round a jarring world they roll,
Still find them happy ; and consenting Spring
Sheds her own rosy garland on their heads :
Till evening comes at last, serene and mild ;
When after the long vernal day of life,
Enamoured more, as more remembrance swells
With many a proof of recollected love,
Together down they sink, in social sleep ;
Together freed, their gentle spirits fly
To scenes where love and bliss immortal
    reign.

95

THE END.